BETWEEN DOG AND WOLF

by Cris Eli Blak

BETWEEN DOG AND WOLF

SPECIAL NOTE

SPECIAL NOTE ON SONGS AND RECORDINGS

Cover Art Design: Morcoil
Book Design: Jonathan Cook
Second Edition: March 2025
ISBN 978-1-964045-03-0

I would like to acknowledge facts. Each day 12 children die from gun violence in America. Guns are the leading cause of death among American children and teens. In 2022, more than 43,000 children were exposed to gunfire at school. Since Columbine in 1999, more than 338,000 students in the U.S. have experienced gun violence at school. That is the only reason this play exists, because school shootings and incidents of in-school violence have continued with no decline. As you read this, let me say I would rather this play not exist.

Thank you to my family. My mother, who is my lighthouse, who gave me permission to dream, who I owe everything to and who is the only reason I am here today. To my grandparents and my sister. And to my aunt and great uncle, who are my guardian angels. To the friends who double as family, who motivate me and push me and say my name in rooms I'm not present in. And to the higher power that keeps gifting me chances at getting this life thing right. I'll get it down one of these days.

And to you, reader, for picking up a play of all things (or even crazier, buying one). Thank you for keeping our craft, and my career, alive. You are appreciated.

-   CEB

BETWEEN DOG AND WOLF by Cris Eli Blak was
originally written and workshopped by Theatre of NOTE in
Los Angeles, as part of their Voices of NOTE workshop
series in March 2021, which culminated in a one-night
reading of the play directed by Rondrell McCormick,
starring:

BLAKE .... Diosiq Burne
PATRICK .... Alexis DeLaRosa
MARA .... Jenny Soo

BETWEEN DOG AND WOLF was announced as the
winner of the 2024 Charles M. Getchell New Play Award
by the Southeastern Theatre Conference.

BETWEEN DOG AND WOLF

CHARACTERS

BLAKE
28, Black male.

PATRICK
28, Latino male.

MARA
27, Black/Latina/Asian female.

PLACE
Small town U.S.A.

TIME
Present Day. Ten years after a school shooting at a local high school. The day before the high school class reunion.

<u>PART ONE</u>

A hotel room.

Nothing luxury, just your typical, in the middle of a city-hotel. Sitting center are two beds, well made up. A table sits between them, a lamp sitting on it. On stage left there is a bathroom area (a toilet and a sink) and to stage right is a door entering into the room. We can hear passing cars from outside - - honking horns, quick radio tunes going past.

Patrick enters, dressed too nice to be called casual but too modest to be called fancy. He is somewhere in-between. He rolls his suitcase beside him, closing the door with his free hand, the key behind his ear.

He lets go of the suitcase and looks around the room, not completely impressed by the room. His eyes ping-pong back and forth to the two beds. He sets his room key down on the table between the beds and walks over to the bathroom, peeking in. He tilts his head to the side - - a silent way of stating, "Good enough, I guess."

Patrick walks over to the bed closest to the door and

sits down.

Quiet.

After the moment of rest, Blake opens the door, an overstuffed backpack hanging off his shoulders, his room key in his mouth. He uses his foot (clothed in a dirt-stained tennis shoe) to kick the door closed. Patrick stands at the sight of him.

BLAKE. Well would you look at this shit here.

PATRICK. Hey Blake.

BLAKE. Patty Martin. All grown up. Come here, baby.

(He drops his backpack to the floor. It creates a thud. He opens his arms, charging Patrick into a bear hug, picking him up. Patrick looks less than enthused.)

PATRICK. It's nice to see you too.

(Blake puts him down.)

BLAKE. Look at us. Old men.

PATRICK. We're not.

BLAKE. Pretty much. Dude, we're here for our high school reunion. That's top tier old man shit.

PATRICK. I'm almost thirty.

BLAKE. Same.

PATRICK. That's not old.

BLAKE. Brother, I am twenty-eight and you are...?

PATRICK. Twenty-eight.

BLAKE. Twenty-eight years of age. That is how old my parents were when they had me. It's not eighteen.

(Blake lies down on the bed closer to the door. Patrick sits down beside him.)

PATRICK. We haven't been eighteen in a long time.

BLAKE. You got that right.

(Sits up.)

So!

PATRICK. So?

BLAKE. What do you think?

PATRICK. ...of what?

BLAKE. The room.

PATRICK. I think it's a room.

BLAKE. But is it a nice room? Do you think the room is nice?

PATRICK. I think that it is a regular hotel room.

BLAKE. Oh.

(He stands up, stuffing his hands in his pockets.)

PATRICK. I didn't mean anything by it.

BLAKE. It's cool, man.

PATRICK. I like the room.

BLAKE. You don't have to say that.

PATRICK. I do. Honest.

BLAKE. Cool. Yeah. No, I get it. I haven't stayed in a lot of hotels in my life. Probably only two. One for a family vacation and one when my family was headed out of town for a funeral. I have a peace sign worth of hotel experience, so for all I know this is the shittiest hotel on the planet.

PATRICK. It's not.

BLAKE. It's not the best either.

PATRICK. I don't know.

BLAKE. Yeah you do.

PATRICK. It's nice. I like it. It's a nice room. I am confused though.

BLAKE. About?

PATRICK. The beds.

BLAKE. The beds.

PATRICK. Yeah.

BLAKE. What about 'em?

PATRICK. Well.

BLAKE. Yeah?

PATRICK. I'm just - -

BLAKE. Confused.

PATRICK. Right.

BLAKE. Yeah you said that.

PATRICK. I know.

BLAKE. You've said you're confused twice now but zero times have you said what you're so confused about.

PATRICK. The beds.

BLAKE. Uh-huh.

PATRICK. There's only two of them.

BLAKE. Wait.

PATRICK. What?

BLAKE. Lemme get this right. You're telling me that there's two beds in this room?!

PATRICK. You're kidding.

BLAKE. I could have sworn I saw ten of them!

(Laughs.)

Come on, bro, when'd you get so stuck up?

PATRICK. I'm not.

BLAKE. You used to know how to take a joke.

PATRICK. It wasn't funny.

BLAKE. Oh! Okay, I'll let that one slide.

PATRICK. The beds though.

BLAKE. There's two of them, I see that.

PATRICK. Did something happen?

BLAKE. Did something happen to what?

PATRICK. To Mara.

BLAKE. You mean, like, did she die?

PATRICK. Is she still coming?

BLAKE. As far as I know.

PATRICK. So shouldn't there be an additional bed?

BLAKE. What's the problem?

PATRICK. It was your job to book the room.

BLAKE. I wouldn't call it a job. No one paid me.

PATRICK. It was your responsibility.

BLAKE. Don't blow a fuse, Pat.

PATRICK. I'm a man now. A grown man. I would prefer it if you only strictly called me by Patrick. That's my name.

BLAKE. Oh your grown man name?

PATRICK. My only name.

BLAKE. Fine, Patrick.

PATRICK. I'll go down to the front desk to see if they have a different room, at least one with a couch.

BLAKE. It's not a big deal.

PATRICK. What, did you plan to put someone on the floor?

BLAKE. Of course not.

PATRICK. In the hallway?

BLAKE. Someone can pair up.

PATRICK. Sleep together.

BLAKE. We're all adults.

PATRICK. I don't know if that's appropriate.

BLAKE. No one said you had to sleep with her. You can bunk with me.

PATRICK. I prefer to have my own space.

BLAKE. One weekend.

PATRICK. I don't know.

BLAKE. You can't go one weekend beside me?

PATRICK. It's not about you. It's just the kind of person I am.

BLAKE. Bullshit. Since when?

PATRICK. I don't know.

BLAKE. One weekend - - not even a full weekend - - being beside me is such a fucking crime to you? I remember basically showering right next to each other in the locker room after practice one day.

PATRICK. Don't bring that kind of stuff up.

BLAKE. What kind of "stuff"?

PATRICK. Stuff...like that.

BLAKE. Why not? You have a problem with the truth? It's what happened. Fucking live with it. Learn to laugh about it.

PATRICK. I don't like it. I don't like hearing about it. I don't like talking about it.

BLAKE. You didn't think it was too much of a problem back in the day.

PATRICK. We were kids.

BLAKE. We were sixteen. Patrick. We had fully formed balls. I saw yours. I know you saw mine, you know what I mean? I know you saw that elephant trunk! What I'm saying is that no one cared. You shouldn't care now.

PATRICK. Fine. I'll put a blanket on the floor. Everybody wins.

BLAKE. Or, you can take a bed and I can take a bed and Mara can be on the floor.

PATRICK. No.

BLAKE. She's the last to arrive. First come, first serve. Survival of the fittest. It's how things work.

PATRICK. It's not. Why don't you take the floor?

BLAKE. I paid for the room.

PATRICK. The wrong room.

BLAKE. The right room, just not the one that's up to your new standards.

PATRICK. Wanting to be able to roll over and not be blocked by the wall of another person is not a standard.

BLAKE. I'll take the floor.

PATRICK. I don't have a problem with it.

BLAKE. Take the bed.

PATRICK. Are you sure?

BLAKE. Your throne awaits.

PATRICK. Thank you.

(He sits on the bed closest to the bathroom.)

BLAKE. And you choose that one?

PATRICK. What's wrong with it?

(Blake shrugs.)

They look exactly the same.

BLAKE. I'm pretty sure they are the same.

PATRICK. Exactly.

BLAKE. But that one's closest to the piss-room.

PATRICK. Yeah?

BLAKE. You have the choice between two beds and you choose the one that's closest to where people take a shit. What if someone has to drop a deuce in the middle of the night and then you have to smell it until morning?

PATRICK. It's just one weekend, right?

BLAKE. Touché. So your opinion of the room itself isn't too high.

PATRICK. Are we not over this?

BLAKE. Let me finish my thought. What about the perks though? Because there are perks.

PATRICK. The perks, such as the free breakfast?

(Blake places his hand on his chest, flattered, honored.)

BLAKE. You motherfucker. You're gonna make me tear up. I knew we were still on the same wavelength. Yes! The free fucking breakfast!

PATRICK. You've always had a thing for breakfast.

BLAKE. It's the most important meal of the day! Oh but my old friend, the breakfast here is no ordinary breakfast.

(He climbs on top of one of the beds.)

It is the breakfast of all breakfasts.

(He starts bouncing on the bed.)

Waffles AND pancakes AND cereal AND muffins AND bacon AND sausage AND eggs AND toast AND oatmeal AND fruit, if you're into that kind of thing.

(He stops bouncing.)

Now you may be thinking, "Well all that food sounds great but I'll surely be thirsty afterwards." No worries! Because this joint is equipped with every liquid you can safely consume in the morning. Are you one of those weird water-only people? We got the clearest in the state. Orange juice. Grape juice. Apple juice. Fuckin' pineapple juice. Papaya! You can get Sprite out the machine if you're so inclined. It is paradise. It is heaven on earth and we are lucky enough to be right in the middle of it.

(He jumps off the bed and stands right in front of Patrick, places his hands on his shoulders. They look right in each other's eyes.)

We are right in the middle of it.

(They stay staring at each other for another beat before snapping back into reality. Patrick backs away, sounding his best fake laugh.)

PATRICK. Yeah well it's good to know you haven't changed.

BLAKE. I like to think I have.

PATRICK. Good.

(He takes out his phone and starts texting.)

BLAKE. Come on...

PATRICK. *(typing on his phone)* What?

BLAKE. None of that.

PATRICK. What?

BLAKE. The phone, bro. The phone. The typing. The texting. Can't we just...be, for now? Be here. Be now. Be this.

PATRICK. It's just that - - you have a phone too.

BLAKE. You don't see it in my hands. You don't even see the imprint in my pockets. I left it in the car.

PATRICK. Aren't you worried about it getting stolen?

BLAKE. Nobody wants my phone, bro.

PATRICK. Thieves don't care who the phone belongs to.

BLAKE. They don't want mine. It isn't all big and nice and shiny and shit.

PATRICK. Okay...

BLAKE. It's a flip.

PATRICK. Your phone is a flip phone.

BLAKE. You have something to say about it?

PATRICK. No. It doesn't matter.

BLAKE. I didn't think so.

(They sit on a bed, turned away from each other for reasons even they can't explain. Patrick puts his phone in his pocket. Silence stings them again.)

It was the cheapest...

PATRICK. What was?

BLAKE. Everything. The room. The phone. They were the cheapest I could find.

PATRICK. Oh.

BLAKE. I kinda fell on hard times, you know, so I had to do

what I could with what I had.

PATRICK. I could have paid for the room.

BLAKE. The room's fine.

PATRICK. I know, but - -

BLAKE. The room was my responsibility, right?

PATRICK. Sure but I didn't know what was going on.

BLAKE. Do you know what's going on or did I tell you I fell on hard times?

PATRICK. The latter. I'm sorry.

BLAKE. I don't need help or sympathy or charity. I got the room. It's not the room people may dream of but it was the cheapest they had and the place I work - the storage facility - gets a discount so I got off pretty fair. And as for the phone, well, I don't really have a reason to have a big flashy phone like yours. That's all for show. If I need to use the internet I can find a computer.

PATRICK. That's smart.

BLAKE. Yeah thanks.

PATRICK. No problem. So, you said a storage facility.

BLAKE. Yup.

PATRICK. What do you do there?

BLAKE. I work.

PATRICK. Right but - -

BLAKE. I sit at the desk. The front desk. Make sure no one's sleeping in their storage, make sure no one stays after closing.

PATRICK. Sounds like an important job.

BLAKE. Is that sarcasm?

PATRICK. No.

BLAKE. It's a job. That's all it is. What about you, big spender? Ten years, a lot has probably happened for you.

PATRICK. I don't know if I'd say that.

BLAKE. Ah. You're one of those.

PATRICK. One of - -

BLAKE. Those fake humble people.

PATRICK. Fake humble people?

BLAKE. Yeah, man, you know, like those celebrities who act like they're the most selfless fucking people on the planet but they can't stop talking about how selfless they are. Like, "I do so much for charity, aren't I the best?" Shit like that. Like you say you don't wanna talk about something but only because you know that if you talked about everything you'd sound pompous.

PATRICK. Nice word.

BLAKE. I'm not stupid.

PATRICK. I was being funny.

BLAKE. Tell me what's been going on. Ten years. A lot to tell.

PATRICK. Should we wait for Mara to come? Then we can have one big communal catch up.

BLAKE. She'll be fine. You know, I was hoping to see you a couple years back at Wiley's funeral.

PATRICK. Oh yeah. Right. I was upset that I had to miss that. So messed up.

BLAKE. He was drunk driving on the wrong side of the road. What'd he expect?

PATRICK. Still tragic.

BLAKE. Yeah. It was a nice funeral. His sister played the

violin. Peyton. That was it.

PATRICK. That's nice.

BLAKE. Didn't you screw her?

PATRICK. Dude.

BLAKE. He's dead, not her. You did though, right? That's crazy. I wonder if he knew. I wonder if when you die you go up to wherever and are told all the secrets you didn't know, like how your teammate railed your sister behind the soccer goal.

PATRICK. Can we talk about something else?

BLAKE. In broad daylight too!

PATRICK. Blake.

BLAKE. It was brave. Real brave. I salute you.

PATRICK. Please respect the fact that I don't want to talk about this.

BLAKE. Did you love him?

(Patrick stands.)

Did you love her?

PATRICK. Stop.

BLAKE. I mean you must have, the way you knocked her up.

(Patrick charges at Blake, who stands up in defense. Patrick pushes him, then pulls him in by the collar of his shirt. We can only hear their breathing. Patrick is red. His eyes are fireballs waiting to cause havoc. Blake has become a child, hands up, afraid. Patrick calms, his color returning to normal. He lets go of Blake, knowing

he has gone to a place he did not intend to. He uses his hand to straighten Blake's shirt then backs away.)

PATRICK. I'm sorry.

BLAKE. I was just being funny.

PATRICK. I didn't find it funny.

BLAKE. I picked that up.

PATRICK. I'm engaged.

BLAKE. To a woman?

PATRICK. What's that supposed to mean?

BLAKE. Congratulations.

PATRICK. Thank you. I want you to be there.

BLAKE. Is this my invitation?

PATRICK. We're getting married in Hawaii. In five months.

BLAKE. Sounds nice.

PATRICK. Her name is Jo.

BLAKE. Joe? And you did say this was a woman, correct?

PATRICK. Jo. Without the E. Short for - -

BLAKE. Not Scarlett Jo-hansson, I'm assuming.

PATRICK. No. Here.

(He pulls out his phone.)

BLAKE. I thought we had an agreement.

(Patrick walks over to Blake and shows him a picture on his phone.)

PATRICK. This is her.

BLAKE. She's very nice looking.

PATRICK. Thank you.

BLAKE. Hawaii sounds nice too.

PATRICK. It is. She has family there.

BLAKE. And you want me to come.

PATRICK. Yes.

BLAKE. Why?

PATRICK. You're my friend.

BLAKE. I'm your high school friend. That's hardly best man material. Though I am honored.

PATRICK. I never said you were going to be my best man.

BLAKE. Then who will be?

PATRICK. My brother.

BLAKE. What the fuck has he done to deserve that?

(Patrick tries to hold in his laugh and keep a straight face. He cracks.)

PATRICK. You're annoying.

BLAKE. So you're engaged. Good to know.

PATRICK. I'd really love for you to be there.

BLAKE. I'll try.

PATRICK. But you can't talk about certain things, okay?

BLAKE. Like you knocking up dead Wiley's sister on the soccer field? Affirmative.

PATRICK. You're a crazy person.

BLAKE. I'm the same me I've always been.

PATRICK. What about you?

BLAKE. What about me?

PATRICK. You haven't found "the one" yet?

BLAKE. You know me.

PATRICK. Surely you've grown - -

BLAKE. Comfortable? Nah. I haven't. I'm not sure it works that way.

PATRICK. I thought maybe - -

BLAKE. You thought maybe shit was just resolved, just like that, in the snap of a finger?

PATRICK. I was hoping.

BLAKE. Fuck hope. I live in reality, where there is no hope.

PATRICK. Only pessimism.

BLAKE. Honesty. Can we pivot?

PATRICK. If we must.

BLAKE. What do you do, for paper?

PATRICK. I'm a teacher. Third grade.

BLAKE. Pay well?

PATRICK. No. Well enough. Kind of. The reward isn't in the check, it's the children.

BLAKE. You smell that?

PATRICK. What?

BLAKE. Bull-shit.

PATRICK. I enjoy my work.

BLAKE. The way you used to talk shit about teachers and now you are one. That's like a felon becoming a cop.

PATRICK. You never heard me talk about my third-grade teacher.

BLAKE. I had a crush on my third-grade teacher.

PATRICK. I would never work in a high school, or even a middle school. Third grade is still an age of discovery, where they're sponge-like, taking it all in and finding who they're going to be, at least for the next couple of years.

BLAKE. Are you a teacher or a psychologist?

PATRICK. I think you have to be both to do a decent job. Kids are hard to understand.

BLAKE. So you work in a school.

PATRICK. Yeah.

BLAKE. Don't you find it ironic?

PATRICK. No.

BLAKE. Not in the least?

PATRICK. Why would I?

BLAKE. Oh. Never mind.

PATRICK. No, what?

BLAKE. I felt like we were going to spend our time back here avoiding certain conversations and now I know I was right.

PATRICK. I'm not avoiding anything.

BLAKE. Sure about that?

PATRICK. Very.

BLAKE. You don't find working in a school to be ironic, or possibly, since we're playing psychologists here, to be some form of redemption for you?

PATRICK. If you have something, say it straight.

BLAKE. You know.

PATRICK. I want you to say it. Communicate your point.

BLAKE. I'm not one of your classroom kids.

PATRICK. You're more like the class bully.

BLAKE. I'm not him either.

PATRICK. Our classroom bully is a girl. A scary, mean little girl. Chemical imbalance at its best. You're not a kid, I know, so don't beat around the bush like one.

BLAKE. Wasn't it hard for you to come here tonight? Didn't you think about turning around and hitting it home the entire time? You had to. I did. I wouldn't be surprised if Mara was in her bed right now in full fetal position 'cause she couldn't bare her bones to show up. Does your pretty little fiancée with the man's name know your story? Our story? The story? I can tell by your face that she doesn't. She doesn't. Does she? Does she?! And you work in a school. Because you're Mr. fucking Rogers now? No. I don't buy that. And you shouldn't be trying to sell it. We're going to a reunion at a school that almost murdered us, Patrick. Such a shame that Wiley was drunk on the wrong side of the road. Boo-hoo. I wasn't surprised when I got the news. He probably had to drink. He saw his best fucking friend get his head blown off. Just like we saw a few people we knew get theirs blown off. But right, let's move on and act like nothing's wrong. Like that motherfucker didn't come into our school and let loose. No one gave a damn then except the people who were there and now you act like it never happened.

PATRICK. Of course it happened. I remember. Of course I do.

BLAKE. Then talk about it.

PATRICK. No.

BLAKE. What a shame. All those brains and you still don't know how to properly process shit.

PATRICK. I'd rather leave the past in the past.

BLAKE. All of it?

(Patrick shoots him a glance, something burning in both of their souls.)

PATRICK. All of it.

BLAKE. I thought you had changed.

PATRICK. I have. From the looks of it I'm the only one.

BLAKE. I'm not sure you have though, bud. You're still a very good liar.

PATRICK. I'm not a liar.

BLAKE. Anymore?

PATRICK. I'm not.

BLAKE. Liar or fraud? Which do you prefer?

PATRICK. I prefer 'Patrick.'

BLAKE. I could see why it would be hard for you to understand. After all, at this point the only person you're lying to is yourself.

(Blake sits back down on the bed closest to the door.)

PATRICK. This was a mistake.

BLAKE. Now you think it was a mistake.

PATRICK. This whole thing.

(He grabs his suitcase.)

BLAKE. Where are you going?

PATRICK. Home. This isn't what I came here for.

BLAKE. It's late.

PATRICK. That just means I'll be home by morning. In my own bed beside someone who doesn't try to make me feel like a douchebag.

BLAKE. It's dark.

PATRICK. Thanks. I didn't know it got dark at night. Look at the big brains on Blake.

(He wheels his suitcase to the door.)

BLAKE. You can't see in the dark.

(Patrick turns around.)

You can't see too well out your one eye. I think it's the...left one. From when you fell onto a piece of metal as a kid. Right? Yeah, I think it's your...left eye. That's why you got here before anyone else, probably right at sundown. You probably planned your entire trip to the minute, didn't you?

(Smiles.)

PATRICK. *(sighs)* I'll get my own room.

BLAKE. Coolio. You should wait here, for a little bit longer, just until Mara gets here. If she's coming. Wait for a bit and you can go get your own room after we all get each other up to date on life. I'm not holding you hostage, just a choice.

PATRICK. *(pause; consideration)* I'll call her and see where she is. If she picks up and is coming and is close, I will wait. We can order some food, eat, talk, be civil human beings.

BLAKE. I love a good ol' fashioned compromise.

(Patrick pulls his phone out again.)

You can't go two minutes without holding that thing in your hand, can you? Where's it gonna run away to? I'm intrigued.

PATRICK. I said I was going to call Mara.

BLAKE. I heard you.

PATRICK. We need to set ground rules first.

BLAKE. I'm all ears, coach.

PATRICK. Keep the conversations appropriate and not, you know, triggering.

BLAKE. For lack of a better word.

PATRICK. I guess.

BLAKE. You got it, captain.

PATRICK. Good.

BLAKE. Gravy.

PATRICK. I'm gonna step out in the hall and make this call. I don't get great service in here.

BLAKE. You're a grown ass man. If you need to step out to make a phone call, step out and make a phone call.

PATRICK. Okay.

(Patrick steps out. Blake walks over to the bathroom, his head turning in the direction of the door. He covers his face with his hands, shakes his head, then lowers them. He turns and also walks out of the room.)

Lights down.

PART TWO

The hotel room, one hour later. Patrick sits on the edge of the bed closest to the bathroom. He impatiently pats on his knees, playing the DIY-drums. He looks over to Blake's backpack, which is sitting idly. Shakes his head. Not a good idea. Waste of a thought.

He continues sitting, reaches in his pocket, and pulls out his phone. He holds it horizontally and starts playing a racing game, his whole body moving left, right, or forward with the movement of the virtual car he's driving.

PATRICK. Dang.

(He crashes. Gives up. Puts his phone back in his pocket, starts drumming again. Looks to the backpack. Fuck it. He walks over to it and stands over it, looking down. To open or not to open, that is the question. The door opens, spooking Patrick back a few steps. Mara enters, dressed the most comfortable and casual of them all, in sweatpants and a large hoodie (hood over her head). She has a shoulder bag that is runneth over with clothes, her room key in one hand, a bottle of

*champagne in the other. She looks at Patrick looking at
the backpack.)*

MARA. Are you gonna ask it to dance with you?

PATRICK. No. It's - - hi.

MARA. Hey.

*(They don't know what to do next. Hug? Handshake?
They nervously laugh.)*

PATRICK. How was the trip?

MARA. The trip. Long.

PATRICK. I bet, with you living at the top of the world.

MARA. I like Maine. Maine is quiet.

PATRICK. Maine is white.

MARA. Yeah but it's the quiet kind of white.

PATRICK. Now it sounds like paradise.

MARA. You never had a good poker face, Patrick.

PATRICK. I've been told. Did you see Blake when you
came in?

MARA. Not that I know of. I haven't seen the guy in ten
years, how the hell am I supposed to know if I passed
him or not? I saw a guy who looked about six hundred
pounds with a bald spot in the lobby. Any chance that's
him? He did look at me for an awfully long time.

PATRICK. I think that may have just been a creep.

MARA. I always get Blake and random creeps confused.

(More laughs.)

PATRICK. It's good to see you.

MARA. You too. You look good.

PATRICK. Yeah thanks. You too. I see you brought some liquid pleasure.

MARA. I figured we'd need it.

PATRICK. You and Blake have fun.

MARA. It's enough for three.

PATRICK. No thanks.

MARA. Whoa. Are you not Patrick Martin? Am I in the wrong room?

PATRICK. Funny. It is me. I just don't drink.

MARA. All grown up.

PATRICK. One might say.

MARA. But grownups aren't afraid of a little champagne.

PATRICK. I'm not afraid. I just stopped drinking.

MARA. Alright. That's good. I probably should. Don't get me wrong, I'm not a boozy floozy or anything, but I enjoy partaking every now and then.

PATRICK. And I am not going to stop you. I'll be watching from the bench.

MARA. You've always been so sweet.

PATRICK. Sure.

MARA. What universal force convinced us all to come back here?

PATRICK. I've been trying to figure that one out myself.

MARA. It's insanity. We're unstable individuals.

PATRICK. Maybe that's why we're here.

MARA. Right. We're nuts.

PATRICK. We have unresolved issues. With the city. With

the school. With each other.

MARA. We're old friends.

PATRICK. We're survivors. We stopped being friends a long time ago.

MARA. Good God, Patrick, we couldn't have started this conversation after I popped the bottle?

PATRICK. You're right. My bad.

MARA. You're not wrong.

PATRICK. I don't want to talk about it either.

MARA. I know something we can talk about. Am I missing something?

PATRICK. I'm not sure...are you?

MARA. Does an extra bed come down from out of the ceiling?

PATRICK. Oh. That was a Blake mistake.

MARA. Typical.

PATRICK. I'll be getting my own room.

MARA. Yeah I might too. Try to get one close just in case I need somewhere to run.

PATRICK. Will try.

MARA. Did you check for bed bugs?

PATRICK. Is that a thing?

MARA. It's what my family always does when we stay at places that aren't our own home. You always have to check. Did you even read the reviews on this place?

(She starts stripping the beds, examining the blankets, sheets, pillows, and pillowcases closely. She moves from one bed to another as the conversation goes on.)

PATRICK. Living in Maine has turned you into a soccer mom.

MARA. If that's what you call someone who doesn't want to catch a parasite then label me whatever the hell you want. Plus, on the bright side - -

PATRICK. The bright side of bed bugs?

MARA. If you do happen to find something you are almost guaranteed at least a hefty discount. Threaten a lawsuit and you might walk away owning the place.

PATRICK. Smooth operator.

MARA. I try.

(She finishes her inspection.)

PATRICK. Find anything?

MARA. Nope. Unfortunately this room is free of bed bugs. Did you check the bathroom?

PATRICK. Be my guest.

(She makes her way there, continuing the conversation.)

MARA. You don't think Blake ran out on us, do you?

PATRICK. I doubt it. He was happier than anyone to be here. I don't think he's too far removed from high school.

MARA. Can you blame him?

PATRICK. Yes. I can.

MARA. Shit took a toll on all of us.

PATRICK. We're pretty well-adjusted, I'd say.

MARA. Outside smiles don't mean crap compared to

internal fires. It'll boil your insides and not apologize after.

PATRICK. That's no excuse for being - -

MARA. Traumatized?

PATRICK. A man-child.

MARA. Having your last drip of childhood stripped away from you in a literal flash is no excuse to be stuck, or, try to harbor yourself in childhood? Get a grip.

PATRICK. Fine. Defend him.

MARA. I'm defending, you're pretending.

PATRICK. Pretending what?

MARA. That you're Superman with feelings of steel.

PATRICK. I'm not.

MARA. I didn't say you were good at pretending. But you're trying.

PATRICK. Isn't trying noble?

MARA. Yeah, if you're not killing yourself in the process.

PATRICK. That's a bit hyperbolic.

MARA. It's a fact.

PATRICK. According to you.

MARA. Do you really expect people to believe that you were somehow the only one spared from being fucked up? Between you and me. You're damaged goods too. Aren't you?

PATRICK. Please. One night. I wouldn't have come if I thought this was going to turn into some kind of intervention.

MARA. It's not. I just wanna know what you're trying to prove to...someone. When we go into that school - when we walk in - no one is going to look at you and say,

"Wow, Patrick is really healthy and well, good for him."
No, if you walk in there and do this - this act - they'll
roll their eyes and say, "Same ol' Patrick, so full of shit
and unaware about how to get it all out." Everyone in
there - in that gym - is going to be reliving their own
personal hells. No one's going to be okay. No one's
going to be paying attention to the music or the
throwback yearbook pictures on a janky ass projector
screen. It's a fragile facade that no one is going to fall
for, just like they're not gonna fall for yours. We're all
mourning all over again. Every street corner and corner
store and storefront has a memory that'll never be
forgotten, no matter how we wish it could be. Believe it
or not...like it or not...we all died that day. We all got a
bullet clean in our chests. And it's still there. It's still
there, Patrick. Do you feel it? Do you ever wake up to
something falling and think you're right back in that
hallway? Or did it really just all go away? Is that what
you want me to believe? If that's what you want me to
believe then I won't bring it up again. Scout's honor.
You tell me.

*(Patrick doesn't move, or speak. He lowers his head,
solemn or ashamed.)*

I thought so.

*(She throws herself beside him on the bed, lying on her
back, stretched out.)*

The ceiling has a crack in it.

(Patrick picks up his head, looks up.)

Do you see it? There's a few.

PATRICK. Yeah. Are you gonna report it?

MARA. I don't know how serious they are with cracks. Depends on how old the building is. If it's ten plus years with no real changes, what can you expect? But if it's still a young one, we may get lucky.

PATRICK. You're the type of person to spill milk in the grocery store then slip on it then try to sue.

MARA. No. Who do you think I am?

PATRICK. Sorry.

MARA. You don't spill it yourself. You bring a friend along with you to do it. Separate cars. There are cameras in stores, you have to be smart.

PATRICK. You'll have to forgive my inexperience.

MARA. Did you ever look at the stars at night when you were a kid?

PATRICK. You did?

MARA. I did. Is that corny?

PATRICK. It's not not corny.

MARA. I'll take it. It's just something about lying on your back and looking at the sky become a light show.

PATRICK. So what you're saying is you've always liked lying on your back.

(She sits up and punches his back up to his shoulder.)

MARA. I can't even have a moment with you!

PATRICK. It was right there, I couldn't pass it up.

MARA. Now the real Patrick shows back up. The old one.

PATRICK. I made one joke.

MARA. One dirty joke.

PATRICK. You're assuming it was dirty. Plenty of people lie on their backs, for a multitude of reasons.

MARA. Example.

PATRICK. Well...

MARA. I'm waiting.

PATRICK. People on the beach wanting a frontal tan.

MARA. That's all you could come up with?

PATRICK. I didn't think it was horrible.

MARA. Horrible may be an understatement.

(She stands up. Patrick, seemingly by instinct, reaches and grabs her hand, pulling her back. Mara looks at him, smiling but in a balance of different emotions.)

PATRICK. I don't know why I did that.

MARA. And yet you're still doing it.

PATRICK. Sorry.

(He lets go. Years of history falling like dust in between them.)

MARA. I remember the last time I was in a room alone with you.

PATRICK. I was messed up that day.

MARA. So was I. And you knew it.

PATRICK. It was a lapse of judgment.

MARA. And what you just did, what would you call that?

PATRICK. I'm not sure. Do I owe you an apology?

MARA. No. You don't. Dinner would be nice. I haven't eaten since this morning.

PATRICK. I was going to wait for Blake to come back.

MARA. Fifteen minutes. I'll give him fifteen minutes. If he's not back in fifteen minutes we fend for ourselves.

PATRICK. Fair deal.

MARA. *(pause)* What are you thinking?

(She sits down on the opposing bed.)

PATRICK. If we're really blasting to the past, maybe a loaded pizza?

MARA. I meant in general.

PATRICK. I'm thinking about what you said.

MARA. I'm glad.

PATRICK. I'm thinking about my wedding.

MARA. *(unresolved)* I saw something about that...

PATRICK. If I'm holding stuff in, like you said - -

MARA. I wasn't trying to shake you up.

PATRICK. If I'm holding stuff in and causing that fire, what if I blow up at her? What if I make a mistake I can't take back? Even if she doesn't know about it, I will. What if I ruin her because I've always been ruined?

MARA. Deep thoughts.

PATRICK. Fears.

(Mara moves to the bed where he is seated. She takes his hand. They look straight ahead, afraid of what might happen if they make eye contact. And they stay like this. Until...Blake busts through the door, dancing. Mara and Patrick quickly disconnect. She moves to the space in-between the two beds. Blake sees her. His smile grows.)

BLAKE. Now it's a party! Let the threesome begin!

(He kicks the door closed with his foot.)

PATRICK. What happened to the conversation we had about keeping it appropriate?

BLAKE. Can you bend over and spread your cheeks so I can remove whatever stick is up your ass?

(Turns.)

Mara. You don't look a day over sixteen.

MARA. Blakey. You don't look a day over forty-five.

BLAKE. *(to Patrick)* Why can't you be more like her?

PATRICK. I guess I lack the empathy.

MARA. He lacks the cup size.

PATRICK. We were waiting on you to come back so we could order dinner.

BLAKE. Who needs dinner...

(He walks over to the bottle of champagne and picks it up.)

...when you have drinks? Now the cycle is complete.

PATRICK. What cycle?

BLAKE. *(holding up the bottle)* Exhibit A: champagne. Noted?

MARA. Noted.

BLAKE. Exhibit B:

(He pulls a plastic bag filled to the top with marijuana out his back pocket.)

Noted?

PATRICK. That's where you went. To buy illegal substances.

BLAKE. Just imagine it's medicinal.

(He tosses it to Patrick, who quickly lets it drop to the ground.)

PATRICK. I'd rather have food.

BLAKE. Yes. Food is a great idea. We'll be hungry after going through that entire bag.

PATRICK. Where did you even get this?

BLAKE. The kid at the front desk. Did you know they let teenagers work hotel front desks? They do here. I mean, I guess not really - - the girl's eighteen. Cute. Don't look at me, I repeat: she is eighteen. Nice kid. Has an attitude problem. But she came through. She's a senior. I probably don't have to tell you where. I told her all about what happened - - they don't even talk about it to these classes. Do you believe that shit?

PATRICK. You talk like we went to Vietnam.

BLAKE. Worse. At least the fuckers in Vietnam knew they were going to war. We thought we were going to gym class. Anyway. They don't talk about it, don't teach about it. At all. Zilch. What a fuckin' blow in the back. But they do still have that mural up.

MARA. I hate that mural.

BLAKE. You should see it now that the paint is all faded. It looks like a big blob of bullshit.

MARA. Can't wait. Maybe we should take a picture in front of it. Scrapbook it.

PATRICK. That sounds like a nightmare.

MARA. Doesn't it all? I say we skip.

PATRICK. What?

MARA. Fuck it. Let's not go.

PATRICK. We didn't come back down here to not go.

MARA. It's not an obligation. What's the loss if we stay in here? What's the gain if we go? We can have fun and avoid the PTSD.

(She snatches the bottle from Blake.)

PATRICK. I don't care what you two do. I'm going. That's what I came here for.

BLAKE. *(to Mara)* Did he tell you he's a teacher now?

MARA. Holy shit.

BLAKE. Right?!

MARA. Is that some kind of trauma therapy?

BLAKE. Right?!

PATRICK. Is this enjoyable to you?

MARA. What grade does he teach?

PATRICK. I'm right here.

BLAKE. I think second.

PATRICK. Third.

BLAKE. Correction. Third.

MARA. The real booger bastards.

PATRICK. I'll just go pick up dinner.

BLAKE. Again, you can't see. You're not going anywhere, Stevie Wonder.

PATRICK. I'll be fine.

BLAKE. Wouldn't it be ironic in the worst kind of way if it's a car accident that kills you while you're in town?

(Patrick stops to consider. Blake is right. Patrick won't admit it.)

PATRICK. I'm sure they have food in the lobby. The well-lit lobby. Would you like to walk me downstairs to make sure I don't fall?

BLAKE. Kinky.

PATRICK. You're foul.

BLAKE. I have a better idea. You can use that fancy phone of yours and order us something.

MARA. Like. A. Pizza.

BLAKE. Like a pizza. I second that choice.

PATRICK. Fine. I'll order a pizza. Anything else?

MARA. We have drinks.

BLAKE. *(picking up the weed)* And we have dessert.

PATRICK. *(shaking his head)* Grow up.

BLAKE. You can get me some of those cinnamon sticks too if they have 'em!

(Patrick gives a thumbs up as he walks out the room, phone to his ear. The door shuts behind him.)

MARA. And then there were two.

BLAKE. You really do look great.

MARA. Okay cut the crap. Talk to me.

BLAKE. I am.

MARA. How often do you smoke? You brought in a sealed baggie but I smell it on your clothes, Blake. The stench don't lie.

BLAKE. I'm not a chimney, you know, I just occasionally like to - -

MARA. Fade away.

BLAKE. Get high.

MARA. *(pause)* He held my hand.

BLAKE. Who? Patrick?

MARA. Yeah.

BLAKE. How...sweet?

MARA. Shut up. Maybe to an onlooking eye but it didn't feel that way. I don't know if you've ever found a lost kid in a supermarket or something like that, and you have to take them to the front counter so they can get on the loud speaker and tell their mother to come to the front of the store. And while you're walking the kid up they hold onto your hand. But it's not 'cause they trust you, it's not 'cause they know you, they just know someone is there. And that's what they need: someone there. Their hands may be shaking and sweating but they aren't about to let go because then they would go right back to not only being lost and left, but being alone. That's what it felt like when he held my hand. Did he tell you he was engaged?

BLAKE. Yes he did.

MARA. How do you feel about that?

BLAKE. What do you mean?

MARA. Just what I asked.

BLAKE. Good for him.

MARA. That's it?

BLAKE. That's it. Good for him.

MARA. I think it's weird and I expected more of a reaction out of you.

BLAKE. You want me to go crazy over it?

MARA. No, but...something rather than nothing. He just never struck me as a marriage type.

BLAKE. Yeah, well, he's changed.

MARA. Apparently. Engagement. School teacher. I feel like he's gonna buy a zoo next.

(Blake laughs.)

What?

BLAKE. I didn't mean to cut you off but this whole time while looking at you, all I could think of was junior year when you were in that stupid play in school. It was when you were trying new things, after that guy with the crooked ear piercing dumped you.

MARA. I was going through a phase.

BLAKE. The motherfucker was peculiar. Not strange. Not weird. Peculiar. He was in my English class. I'd sit the whole forty-five minutes trying to figure out what the fuck was going through his head.

MARA. I thought he was hot.

BLAKE. A hot ass mess. The man's dandruff was so bad it started forming a colony on his scalp. How'd it feel having him dump you?

MARA. I'm sorry, are we talking about the boy or are we talking about the play?

BLAKE. Oh I'mma talk about the play. You dragged us to go see that shit, even got us discounted tickets. Front row too. That was the weirdest shit I ever saw but everyone in the audience loved it. All five of them. You did good.

MARA. That whole story to, what, call me dramatic?

BLAKE. Maybe.

MARA. I remember some things from junior year too.

BLAKE. Yeah...don't we all...

(Mara picks up her bag and makes her way towards the bathroom.)

MARA. Mind if I shower?

BLAKE. Mi casa es su casa.

MARA. Thanks.

BLAKE. I won't peek.

MARA. I appreciate it. *(stops)* Hey Blake.

BLAKE. 'Sup?

MARA. We haven't seen each other all these years. None of us. We've barely talked. All three of us haven't been in the same place having a conversation for a decade. Why did we stop being friends? And why do I seem to be the only one who cares that we aren't anymore?

BLAKE. What do you want me to say?

MARA. An answer.

BLAKE. One that satisfies you?

MARA. One that's true. You two have your battles to fight with yourselves and that's whatever, but I'm only asking one question here. I don't think that's too much. I think I deserve something.

BLAKE. The most satisfying answer I can give you is, I don't know. Because I don't. Times change. People change. Lives change. Relationships change.

MARA. Not overnight.

BLAKE. They do if earlier that day someone shot up your school. Things change real quick then.

MARA. What if coming back here was the worst decision of our lives?

BLAKE. Once again, I don't know.

MARA. Why are you here?

BLAKE. Why are you?

MARA. To remind myself why I left.

(She enters the bathroom area. Blake sits on the bed closest to the door. As the lights go down we begin to hear the sound of a shower. The shower becomes rainfall.)

PART THREE

About an hour has passed. A half-empty pizza box is on the floor, Blake sitting on the floor beside it. Mara is on the bed closest to the door now while Patrick sits on the one by the bathroom. Blake and Patrick are in the same clothes while Mara is now in their pajamas.

They finish laughing at a joke or story that we did not hear. They pass around a rolled joint, smoke dancing off the tip. Mara passes it to Patrick, who immediately passes it to Blake, who takes a puff. The bottle of champagne is half-empty, paper cups sitting beside each of the friends.

PATRICK. Alright. I think it's time for me to go down and get that room.

MARA. *(thumbs down)* Booooooo!

BLAKE. Come on, man.

PATRICK. It's late.

BLAKE. Just stay here. I said I'd take the floor.

PATRICK. Mara said she was getting her own room too.

MARA. I said I might. But I'm comfortable now.

PATRICK. I still need my space.

MARA. Or! Or! Or! We play a game.

BLAKE. I like it already.

PATRICK. What kind of game?

MARA. *(picking up the bottle)* A drinking game.

PATRICK. Absolutely not.

MARA. This is our only chance. This isn't gonna happen again. For all we know this is the last time we see each other, so why not partake? For once. Then you can fill your cup back up with water, and go back to being whatever you are out there in the real world.

PATRICK. *(pause)* Fine.

BLAKE. Yes! He has returned!

PATRICK. I'm not doing too much.

MARA. Shot straight out the bottle. As much or as little as you want. We respect limits in this room. This is a safe space.

PATRICK. What are the rules?

MARA. No rules. Pure fun. Tell us your favorite high school memory. Any takers?

(There are none.)

I'll go, no worries.

(Drinks.)

My favorite high school memory was skipping lunch to go to McDonald's. And it was that one time where the security lady - - you guys know her. Come on. She drove the golf cart around campus.

(They all start laughing.)

BLAKE. Oh yeah.

PATRICK. We used to call her CSI.

BLAKE. Yes! C-S-I! 'Cause she came back every week and couldn't solve shit!

MARA. It was that one time though, when she caught us driving off. Who was behind the wheel?

BLAKE. Probably me.

PATRICK. Definitely you.

MARA. And she started chasing the car with her golf cart, all the way out onto the highway. That was golden.

PATRICK. I wonder if she still works there.

BLAKE. Doubt it.

MARA. Who's next?

PATRICK. *(to Blake)* I wouldn't make you wait.

BLAKE. You're so full of it, you know that?

(He snatches the bottle, drinks much more than Mara.)

MARA. You can't just hog the bottle, you have to tell us your best memory.

BLAKE. Alright. Uh. Best high school memory. Um. My best high school memory is...damn...

MARA. You have to have one.

PATRICK. At least.

BLAKE. I got it. I got it. Homecoming. Sophomore year.

MARA. Hold on.

PATRICK. We said we weren't talking about that.

BLAKE. It's been long enough.

PATRICK. We took a vow.

MARA. He's right.

BLAKE. Okay. Permission to speak on it. Once.

PATRICK. Permission granted.

BLAKE. Thank you, Pope Patrick. Sophomore year. Homecoming. I'm just out there, on the dance floor, trying my best to look cool, and who taps me on the shoulder?

PATRICK. Trisha Pack.

BLAKE. Trisha motherfucking Pack! Taps on my shoulder and says in that sexy ass Nigerian accent, "You want to dance?" And her dress is breaking every dress code. For hours we dance and she's just, you know, like, grinding on me. By the time the dance is over I'm sore down there from her bumping up on me the entire time. I always say that was the night I lost my virginity.

MARA. Now I remember why we don't talk about it. That's disgusting.

PATRICK. You two danced, that's it.

BLAKE. I know but I was, what, fifteen, sixteen? After about five minutes of her up on me I busted quicker than a tire on a nail.

MARA. *(dry-heaving)* Okay time to pass the bottle.

BLAKE. I wasn't done.

MARA. You're so done. Pass it.

(Blake passes the bottle to Patrick.)

PATRICK. Can't I get some tap from the sink and throw that

back?

MARA. Dude. It's champagne.

BLAKE. Champagne. Basically alcoholic tap water.

(Patrick takes a small sip.)

PATRICK. Good enough?

(Blake and Mara shrug.)

My favorite memory from back then was...I think it was meeting you guys.

MARA. Ew.

BLAKE. Of course you're the one who gets sappy about it.

PATRICK. I'm serious. Before I met you guys I didn't have any friends. I didn't know who I was. I was lonely. Every day was routine. Wake up, go to school, go to class, go to lunch, go back to class, go home. A spinning wheel. You guys took me out of that.

MARA. None of us had anyone before we met. We're a three-piece puzzle that broke apart.

BLAKE. I was always cool.

MARA. Sure you were. Okay, pass it back to me. Now we play the other side. Take a shot, as much or as little as you'd like, straight out the bottle, and say your worst high school experience.

PATRICK. That seems unnecessary.

BLAKE. I think we're all pretty fucking aware of the worst experience.

MARA. That was a collective experience. Everyone in the

student body went through that. I mean an individual experience.

BLAKE. Individually, I still go with that day.

MARA. You didn't take a shot.

BLAKE. I don't need it. I don't need it to think about that day. I was in the gym. The only reason I got out so quickly was 'cause the gym had those emergency exits.

PATRICK. I was in the computer lab. Not as easy.

BLAKE. There was a kid. I never paid much attention to him if I'm being honest. But he was in my gym class. While we all played basketball he just walked along the bleachers, talking to himself. He was there. You know, he was present. But the guy was a ghost. He had this thing about getting changed only after everyone else was out of the locker room and already doing something. I still remember the time I heard the first shot. 9:58. I wake up every morning at 9:58. We were all in the gym, playing ball, doing whatever, but that kid had just gone back in the locker room to get changed and he must have gotten stuck in a stall or I don't know, but he's the only one from class that got killed. And that's fucked up. That's so fucked up. But what's more fucked up is how I still don't know his name. I still don't know his name.

(Takes the bottle.)

Is that a bad enough experience or do I need to make it a little more personal?

MARA. Yeah. I think that'll do.

BLAKE. What about you?

MARA. I won't go with what's easy.

BLAKE. I wouldn't call some kid getting his chest blown open easy.

MARA. I didn't mean it like that. Jesus Christ. I - - mine is when I took Wiley's sister to get her abortion. Peyton.

PATRICK. Why would you bring that up?

MARA. It's my least favorite memory.

PATRICK. I'm sure you had other options.

MARA. Maybe, but it's my turn.

PATRICK. I'm done playing.

BLAKE. You can't run from the past forever, brother.

PATRICK. I'm not your brother.

BLAKE. I thought we saved your life.

PATRICK. I was being nice.

BLAKE. Fuck you. You just can't take the heat.

MARA. Can I ever talk without being cut off?

PATRICK. I don't like the game. I tried to play along but I'm not doing this.

MARA. You didn't see her crying.

PATRICK. I don't care.

MARA. You should.

PATRICK. Why?

MARA. It was your fucking kid.

PATRICK. That's what we think.

MARA. She was younger than us. I doubt she had even ever done...anything, with anyone.

PATRICK. I don't know.

MARA. Wouldn't you though? That girl was really scared and you - - you couldn't even show up. I didn't sleep with her and I was there.

PATRICK. I was busy.

MARA. You weren't too busy to try to sleep with me the same week.

BLAKE. Hello.

PATRICK. I told you I wasn't in the right headspace.

MARA. You seemed pretty aware to me.

PATRICK. I wasn't.

MARA. The whole time we were in that clinic waiting room all she could tell me is how she was sure you were a good guy, how she still liked you. And I had to sit there and listen to it and fight back to urge to tell her what you really were.

PATRICK. Yeah, and what's that?

MARA. An asshole who didn't want anyone to see he was an asshole.

PATRICK. I don't know what you want from me.

MARA. You were scared. Just like you are now. You avoided the tough stuff then and you're dodging it now. Do you ever think about it?

PATRICK. No.

MARA. How?

PATRICK. I told you. I don't care. It's not relevant.

MARA. To who?

PATRICK. To me.

MARA. That kid would almost be a teenager now.

PATRICK. I don't care about the kid! The kid wasn't born so it isn't even a kid. It was an idea. It was a mistake. It was taken care of.

MARA. Taken care of?

PATRICK. There's nothing to talk about. End of story.

BLAKE. You really don't think about it?

PATRICK. I just answered that.

BLAKE. Do you even remember when y'all hooked up?

PATRICK. What kind of question is that? We were kids, that was so long ago - -

BLAKE. So no.

PATRICK. I try not to.

BLAKE. Makes sense.

PATRICK. Oh does it now?

BLAKE. Yeah. Explains why you didn't recognize this place.

PATRICK. What are you talking about?

BLAKE. This is where it happened. Not this exact room. But this hotel.

PATRICK. You said you picked this place because it was cheap.

BLAKE. That too. It was. Cheap as hell.

PATRICK. How do you even know that?

BLAKE. She told me. We went out for drinks after her brother Wiley's funeral. My treat. I asked for the deets, the story, the buzz. After a few drinks, she spilled it all on the bar, baby. All of it. You stole fifty bucks from your pops' wallet and paid for a room here. For the record, she was a virgin. Told me that too.

PATRICK. That's not important to me. She's not important to me.

BLAKE. Who the fuck are you?

(Patrick gets up, grabs at his suitcase again.)

PATRICK. I think you've smoked too much.

BLAKE. That fiancée of yours must be a bitch.

PATRICK. Excuse me?

BLAKE. You heard me. Your fiancée must be a bitch. Should I say it louder?

PATRICK. Take it back.

MARA. He didn't mean it.

BLAKE. I meant it.

PATRICK. He needs to take it back.

(Blake laughs.)

I don't find anything funny. Take it back.

BLAKE. Chill.

PATRICK. Now!

(Blake stands, handing the joint to Mara.)

BLAKE. Okay. I'm sorry. My bad.

PATRICK. Okay.

BLAKE. Your fiancée isn't a bitch. She's just a cunt.

(Patrick pushes Blake. Intoxicated and unbalanced, it causes Blake to trip over himself and fall to the ground.)

MARA. Gentleman!

PATRICK. He started it!

(Blake stands up and rolls up his sleeves.)

Don't talk about my fiancée. You don't even know her. It's out of line.

BLAKE. It's fucked up.

PATRICK. I said that.

BLAKE. No you didn't. Say it. Say it's fucked up.

PATRICK. No.

(Blake pushes Patrick.)

MARA. Dude.

PATRICK. I'm not saying it. I'm not stooping down to your level. Not tonight. I'm better than you. You might not like hearing it but it's true. I am better than you.

(Blake pushes again.)

BLAKE. Say it's fucked up! Say fuck something! Fuck me. Fuck the world. Fuck the fuckin' misery. Fuckin' anything!

(Patrick pushes back.)

PATRICK. No. Back up.

BLAKE. Or what? Huh? That's the second time tonight you tried to pull some shit on me like you're gonna do something. I wish you would. I wish - - follow through, baby! If you wanna do something, do it!

PATRICK. You're not worth it.

BLAKE. I bet you feel good saying that.

PATRICK. As a matter of fact I kind of do, yes.

BLAKE. Yeah I bet. You and this sudden fuckin' superiority shit. You wanna feel big 'cause you're small. You are tiny.

PATRICK. Whatever.

BLAKE. That's all you got?

PATRICK. Get away from me.

MARA. Guys.

(Blake slaps his own face.)

BLAKE. Hit me, motherfucker. You're a man.

MARA. What the fuck?

PATRICK. You need to calm down.

BLAKE. Take a strike!

PATRICK. Calm down!

(Blake slaps himself again.)

BLAKE. Right here!

(He goes to do it again. Mara, joint in mouth, grabs his arm before he can.)

MARA. Stop. Take a fucking breath. Both of you.

(Blake yanks away from her. He points at Patrick, who flinches. Blake laughs.)

BLAKE. I was hoping you'd be a man for once.

PATRICK. I am a man.

BLAKE. Is that what your fiancée tells you? What's her name again?

PATRICK. I told you not to talk about her.

BLAKE. It's not like it matters. Right? You're not gonna do something if I do. I could stand right here in the middle of this room and talk about how I fucked the brains out your future wife. I could say she rode my shit until it was crooked and you wouldn't - -

(Patrick charges Blake, pushing him onto the bed. He begins throwing punches. Blake blocks his face with his arms. Mara pulls Patrick off. Blake, not hurt but out of breath, stands. He claps hard.)

There we go! There we go! That's more like it. Let that fuckin' crazy out.

PATRICK. You're insane.

BLAKE. Damn right. You're damn right I am. So watch out. 'Cause I"m on your ass.

PATRICK. Find something better to do.

BLAKE. Like hide behind some bullshit job title? Go volunteer at the YMCA or some shit.

PATRICK. I do!

BLAKE. Because you're a fucking fake! You are a faker!

PATRICK. Or maybe I've grown! Have you thought of that?

Maybe I am a grown man. An adult. Someone who knows how to process shit and doesn't have to drown myself in a bottle of booze anytime I remember something that isn't pleasant!

(Kicks a cup down.)

GOD!

(Silence. Not able to help himself, he bends over and picks up the cup. This refuels Blake.)

BLAKE. You can't be proud of who you are.

PATRICK. And you can be?

BLAKE. At least I'm real. I may be fucked up but I'm real and don't try to mask it. You are in a costume twenty-four seven and now you don't know how to take it off and just be you. Who cares if you're fucked up? Other fucked up people?

PATRICK. I'm not doing this.

BLAKE. Of course you're not. Because we are different.

PATRICK. Yeah. We are.

BLAKE. We are. You are a dog. A whining, panting, helpless dog. And I am a wolf. Dogs cry until someone else fills their bowl. They're afraid of thunder and feel safe when caged, and hate when they can't smell their owner nearby. They are weak and dependent. Domesticated. Happy with their homes. Wolves don't beg for shit! They go out and they get their own. They chase for what they need to survive and they clamp their jaw on it 'til it's theirs. It's do or die for them, it's feed or be fed upon. It isn't pretty, it isn't cute, but it's a fucking life, and they do what they have to do to keep going another day. We howl at the thunder. We bask in our freedom. We fend for ourselves. You are a dog. Sheep in wolf's clothing have more dignity than you. I am a wolf. We are very close. We are very close in appearance and origin but we could not be more far removed, you blind fuck. You have lost the part of you that is true, that is wild, that is natural. You are in wolf territory right now, brother, and you know it. You are in the deepest darkest depths of the woods, not in a finely cut backyard. So act accordingly, asshole. Or you will get eaten. And whoever you care so dearly about will get over it in due time and get a new dog to lay at the edge of their bed. And you best believe that new puppy is gonna be much bigger than you, with more of a bite.

(Patrick sits in the corner, his hands over his head, rocking back and forth.)

PATRICK. You're an ass.

BLAKE. I know. At least I'm man enough to admit it. What about you?

MARA. Are you two done being animals? Or do you wanna make more noise and get us kicked out?

PATRICK. You don't think I know I'm a failure?

MARA. No one said you were - -

PATRICK. You don't think I know?! You don't think - - you don't think I'm trapped? You don't think my existence, my own soul, suffocates me? How do you know these things?! How can you be sure that you know who I am? I am the way I am because that's the only way I avoid crashing my car against a tree! You don't believe me? On my way here, the way I came, I had to pass the school. I had to drive past it and I didn't know what to do. I didn't know if I should speed as fast as I could to get away from it or cruise around the perimeter of it, take in every stone and brick and sprout of grass. I ended up doing something in the middle. And for a brief second I thought, "Wow, wouldn't it be beautiful if I killed myself right here? If I went on the football field and cried and showed everyone how much crap I was really going through and ended it right there. Wouldn't that be meaningful? Wouldn't it be poetic?" But it's not. It's nothing powerful in letting it win over you. So maybe you're right - - no, you are. I'll give it to you. I am a bottle of a man but I have to survive. I have things to live for and if I dive in the deep end of my head I am going to die. I will literally die. So forgive me for being a dick when I was eighteen and forgive me for being a bad friend when I was seventeen and forgive me for being a liar at twenty-eight. But I don't do it for you, for either of you. For any of you. I do it so my heart doesn't burst inside my body. Yes I hear it too. Like you said, you got out easy. You didn't see all the shit you want people to believe you did. You ran. And good for you. But you didn't see what I saw! You didn't see all the bodies and all the blood that I saw! You didn't come as close as I did! So, yes, it's personal! And it's hard to look you in the eyes when you act like you have the tragic story. Maybe you do but it's not worth a goddamn dime next to mine! No one's is!

MARA. I saw the bodies.

PATRICK. Okay.

MARA. No. It's not okay. I stand here like someone's
    shadow on the wall and listen to you two play volleyball

with your demons and hardly look at me. Ask me if I have a boyfriend. Ask me. Someone. One of you. One of you men. What about me? What about my fucked up memories? What about my pain? Do you even think about that? Have you ever thought about that? Ask me. Neither of you will. Because you know the answer is no. And you know why?

(Pause.)

I don't feel well.

BLAKE. Maybe you should sit down.

MARA. Shut up. I saw my boyfriend die. When he stood in front of me and took a bullet. That's what I hear every night. That's what I see. Being okay is a fucking lie. No one is ever okay. We come out crying because we know that we'll never be comfortable again. We'll never be sure if we're the ones to blame. We're not. We can say it. But we can't convince ourselves to believe it. Thankfully the kids in gym class survived. Did either of you know him? The guy who did it? Like really know him?

PATRICK. Not really.

BLAKE. Not really.

MARA. Not really. But apparently he was getting his ass kicked every day. Like, he ended up in the hospital a couple times 'cause of people who went to school with us.

PATRICK. Am I supposed to care?

MARA. No. Fuck that guy. I hope he's burning on a grill in hell right now. But you're not the only one who's seen things. You're not the only one.

BLAKE. *(pause)* Hand me my bag. My backpack.

PATRICK. Why?

BLAKE. I want to play another game.

(Patrick stands and does as told. Blake sits the bag on the bed closest to him. He unzips it, pulls out a handgun.)

MARA. I can't do this.

(Holding her stomach, she runs into the bathroom.)

PATRICK. We're doing this now?

BLAKE. Let's do Russian Roulette. Best party game right after Spin the Bottle.

PATRICK. Put the gun down. This isn't funny.

BLAKE. I'm not laughing.

(He points the gun at Patrick.)

PATRICK. Blake.

BLAKE. *(lowering the gun)* I carry this everywhere I go. It ain't because I'm some second amendment motherfucker. I need this. Because people are following me, man. Ghosts. Everywhere I go. Haunting me. Taunting me. Sucking my blood. This makes me feel like I've won. If someone had one of these when that fucker came in and started emptying their rounds, a few people may be alive. I'm fighting fire with fire and watching this fucked up world burn. If what happened to us had happened in any other school with any other kind of people it would have been on the fucking History Channel. But because it happened to us - - nobody cares. Not even the school itself. They expect it. A gun in that school with people who look like us? Doesn't matter.

(Looks at gun.)

This is my therapy. It might be wrong. I know it is. But it's the only thing that works for me.

(He puts the gun back in the bag. Mara returns, wiping her mouth.)

MARA. Are you done?

BLAKE. All done.

(They all sit, a distance between each other, none of them even turning to look. A long freeze in time.)

MARA. Are we going? Are we going tomorrow or not? Am I talking to myself?

BLAKE. I don't know.

PATRICK. I am. I came all this way. Might as well.

MARA. I don't know either.

PATRICK. *(rising)* Well. You all have a good amount of hours to decide. I need my space.

(Pause.)

I'll see you at breakfast.

(He grabs his suitcase and exits.)

MARA. *(pause)* Are we gonna be okay?

BLAKE. Are you okay?

MARA. No. I'm far from it.

BLAKE. We're made out of pain. It's planted in our foundation.

MARA. I guess that means no then.

BLAKE. I'm not sure, Mara.

MARA. Looks like we finally see eye-to-eye on something.

BLAKE. First time for everything.

(He begins picking things up from the floor.)

MARA. Should we check on him?

BLAKE. He left on his own.

MARA. And?

BLAKE. And we can't help him.

MARA. We could try.

BLAKE. You can.

MARA. I might.

BLAKE. I assume you'll walk out next to get your own room.

MARA. I think I'll stay here. We each have a bed. Not a problem. No reason to waste money.

BLAKE. Cool.

MARA. I should get some fresh air though. Breathe a little after...all that. You know - -

BLAKE. I get it.

MARA. Wanna join?

BLAKE. No thanks.

MARA. Okay.

(She starts for the door.)

BLAKE. Have you?

MARA. Have I...?

BLAKE. Dated anyone since? In college? At all?

MARA. No. I've tried. Thought about it. But no. I see him every day, his body ripped apart by bullets. We hadn't even been dating that long. I should have died that day. I should have died ten years ago. I'm afraid to have kids, between you and I. I could never drive them to school. They'd hate me. They wouldn't understand.

BLAKE. You don't know that.

MARA. You're optimistic now?

BLAKE. I want one of us to be happy.

MARA. I am. In my own way.

BLAKE. I never thought about any of that - - having kids and stuff.

MARA. Never?

BLAKE. I used to.

MARA. What changed?

BLAKE. I started looking at myself in the mirror and realized I can't look at one of me without getting sick, let alone multiple.

MARA. We are one damaged crew.

BLAKE. Yeah but we have some pretty interesting stories to tell.

MARA. If we do go, you might see Trisha Pack there.

BLAKE. *(laughs)* You think so?

(Mara shrugs.)

MARA. Out of curiosity - -

BLAKE. Yeah?

MARA. If he's a dog and you're a wolf, what does that make me?

BLAKE. *(pause; after thought)* It makes you whatever comes between the two. Whatever holds them together, keeps them in the same family. You're better.

MARA. I'm gonna go get that air.

BLAKE. I'll be here.

MARA. Nice.

(Pause.)

It really is good to see you.

BLAKE. Thanks. It's really good to see you too.

(Mara exits. Blake puts everything he picked up onto the table between the beds. He looks around the room then sits on the bed closest to the door. Pause. He stands and moves over to the one closest to the bathroom. He

stands up on the bed, bounces a little, then drops himself down. He walks over to the bathroom, looks in. He turns and walks to the door. Thinks. He gives the room another look, then exits.)

Lights down.

END OF PLAY

GATHER BY THE GHOST LIGHT

WITH JONATHAN COOK & DEVON MCSHERRY

GATHER BY THE GHOST LIGHT is a storytelling podcast in radio theater format. Think of the Ghost Light as your campfire. Gather around and listen to stories from a variety of genres. Playwright Jonathan Cook and Devon McSherry are the hosts of the series and most of the stories you hear were originally written as short stage plays and they now have been adapted to audio plays with professional voice actors and immersive sound effects. The audio plays produced on this podcast give these talented playwrights an even wider audience for their stories. We welcome you to join us on this journey as we extend the voices of emerging playwrights!

Available wherever you get your podcasts!
For more information, please visit:
www.gatherbytheghostlight.com

Gather by the Ghost Light annual anthologies of audio plays produced on the podcast are all available through Ghost Light Publications!

BOBBY IS DEAD
by Marty Matfess

Chris has been madly in love with his best friend Annie for years, but she's only been interested in dating everyone else but him. After Annie's recent break up with her boyfriend Bobby, Chris feels this may finally be what he needs to find his way into her heart, but just like that ... she's already moved on to another guy she met at a coffee shop. Being the good friend that he is, Chris has agreed to hang out with the new guy's visiting sister while they go out on a date. Oh, and let's not forget about Bobby. Turns out he's not taking the break up too well and Chris is now caught between an aggressive ex-boyfriend while having to keep new guy's sister company. A play about love, lust, and getting shot in the head.

IN THE SLUSH
by Daniel Prillaman

2023 FINALIST FOR NEW DRAMATISTS' PRINCESS GRACE AWARD

Newlywed Laura Beth Gardner has it all. A loving husband, a baby on the way, and a usually delightful job. But this weekend, tasked with reading through her publishing house's slush pile, she encounters a mysterious manuscript that claims she isn't human. That her husband isn't who he says he is. And that she's a vessel for her unborn child, who is actually the Second Coming of an ancient darkness that will devour the world. It has to be some sort of joke.

…But what if it's not?

A cosmic horror about identity, creation, and the things we'll do to realize our dreams.

VERLASSEN
by Avery Lewis

A prisoner awaiting his punishment. A pastor seeking vengeance. A survivor searching for peace. All three are looking to one girl, Ida Verlassen, to give them what they're after. As time works against them and revelations are made, Ida must decide who she trusts, and which direction she will choose to go.

HUGO SAVES CHRISTMAS…IN MAY!
by Steven Hayet

For Maya Kaplan, Christmas is her life… and she hates every minute of it. As acting manager of a year-round Christmas store, Maya is force-fed jolly, subjected to hearing the same holiday songs on loop day after day. Fortunately, Maya's nightmare will be coming to an end in a few months as the store will finally shutter its doors to become a Starbucks. Or will it? Enter Hugo McGee, a longtime customer devastated to learn of the store's closing. Refusing to allow a local intuition to disappear, Hugo makes it his mission to raise the money and keep Yuletide Cheer open, despite Maya's objections.

KINGDUMB
by Jonathan Cook

There's a new King in the land that has initiated a mysterious new tax on the citizens. Outraged, the region's finest Clock fixer, aka "Time Repair Specialist", recruits some of the most unlikely rebels to help him develop a plan to overthrow the King. Their plotting takes them on a comedic journey through perilous mountain tops all the way to the palace itself where they confront this vile King face to face. Kingdumb is a medieval fantasy comedy full of absurdist humor and illogical behavior.

ALL BARK, NO BITE
by Kara Emily Krantz

Charlotte and Eugene live a quiet, no-nonsense lifestyle surrounded by sudoku and argyle. Robert and Bella are boisterous and messy and ridiculously in love. Then there's the neighbor, Suzanne, who basically doesn't know what's going on, but definitely has something to say about it. Sure, relationships can be exciting! They can also be confusing, unexpected, and expose us to profound emotional risk. However, relationships are almost always worth exploring, and if we're willing to be vulnerable, can fill up the empty or wounded spaces in our hearts. And if that doesn't work? Well, get a dog.

CRAZY QUILTS

by Karen Fix Curry

A young woman goes to interview a quilting group and finds herself being interviewed for inclusion in their exclusive secret club. Things are not always what they seem. Strangers can quickly become family, and at her lowest moment can change her life in unexpected, profound, and sometimes unsettling ways.

BARON OF BROWN STREET

by Eric Mansfield

Lenny King, a homeless man living alone in a tent under Akron's Brown Street bridge, becomes an overnight celebrity after a newspaper story details Lenny's kind heart in forgiving three teens who set him on fire and laughed at his pain. Enduring the physical and emotional scars of a man abused by life and his own bad decisions, Lenny must now fend off strangers looking to exploit him for their own publicity and others from his past looking to help him and reconnect. (Inspired by true events.)

THE CHRONICLES OF GREAT BRITAIN'S FIRST EVER VAMPIRE TEDDY BEAR

by Christopher Plumridge

This is the story of a Teddy Bear who became a legend! Detailed across ten adventurous monologues, each one more heroic and entertaining than the last. Through his various exploits you will discover how a simple stuffed toy became the legend that is 'Great Britain's First Ever Vampire Teddy Bear'.

THE DESTINATION

by Ryan Kaminski

In the midst of a blizzard, a group of strangers seek refuge in a secluded motel, unaware that the motel proprietor and a mysterious stranger will make them part of a deadly game. A psychological horror play set during the holiday season.

www.ghostlightpubs.com

www.ingramcontent.com/pod-product-compliance
Lightning Source LLC
Chambersburg PA
CBHW070426310726
48977CB00003B/857